Rules in the Library

Written by Tracey Michele

Picture Dictionary

food and drink

noise

Read the picture dictionary. You will find these words in the book.

return

rip or bend

tidy

Libraries have rules.
They have rules
so that people
can enjoy the library.

Rule 1

No food and drink
in the library.
Food and drink
can damage library books.

Rule 2

Do not be noisy
in the library.
People cannot work
in the library
if you are noisy.

Rule 3

Do not rip or bend library books.
Books cost money.
If you damage a book, you will have to pay for it.

Rule 4

Keep the library tidy.
Put your books back where they came from.
People cannot find books if the library is untidy.

Rule 5

Return your library books on time.
If you do not return your books on time, other people cannot read them.

Activity Page

Write some more rules for the library. Make a poster with your rules on it.

Do you know the dictionary words?